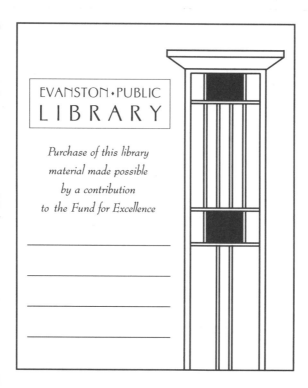

Protecting Habitats

PROTECTING Rain Forests

Moira Butterfield

GARETH STEVENS
GS
PUBLISHING
A Member of the WRC Media Family of Companies

Please visit our web site at: www.garethstevens.com
For a free color catalog describing Gareth Stevens Publishing's list of high-quality books
and multimedia programs, call 1-800-542-2595 (USA) or 1-800-387-3178 (Canada).
Gareth Stevens Publishing's fax: (414) 332-3567.

Library of Congress Cataloging-in-Publication Data

Butterfield, Moira, 1961–
    Protecting rain forests / Moira Butterfield. — North American ed.
    p. cm. — (Protecting habitats)
    Includes index.
    ISBN 0-8368-4994-9 (lib. bdg.)
    1. Rain forests—Juvenile literature. 1. Habitat conservation—Juvenile literature.
  I. Title. II. Series.
  QH86.B88   2005
  577.34—dc22   2005042623

This North American edition first published in 2006 by
Gareth Stevens Publishing
A Member of the WRC Media Family of Companies
330 West Olive Street, Suite 100
Milwaukee, WI 53212 USA

This U.S. edition copyright © 2006 by Gareth Stevens, Inc. Original edition copyright © 2004 by Franklin Watts.
First published in Great Britain in 2004 by Franklin Watts, 96 Leonard Street, London, EC2A 4XD, UK.

Designer: Rita Storey
Editor: Sarah Ridley
Art Director: Jonathan Hair
Editor-in-Chief: John C. Miles
Picture Research: Diana Morris
Map artwork: Ian Thompson
Consultant: Dr Sue Brooks, Birkbeck College, London

Gareth Stevens Editor: Gini Holland
Gareth Stevens Cover Design: Dave Kowalski

Photo credits: Bojan Brecel/Still Pictures: 21; Romain Garrouste/Still Pictures: 4; Ron Giling/Still Pictures: 16;
Herbert Giradet/Still Pictures: 19; P Goetgheluck/Still Pictures: 14; Masahiro Iijima/Ardea: 23;
Martin Jones/Ecoscene: 10; Wayne Lawler/Ecoscene: 5; Luiz C. Marigo/Still Pictures: 25; Ted Mead/Still
Pictures: 7; Minden Pictures/FLPA: 1, 12, 20, 22; Sally Morgan/Ecoscene: 17; NASA/Ecoscene: 26;
Robert Pickett/Papilio/Ecoscene: 11; E Kjell Sandved/Ecoscene: 13; David Woodfall/Still Pictures: 9

Printed in the United States of America

1 2 3 4 5 6 7 8 9 09 08 07 06 05

CONTENTS

All about Rain Forests

Rain forests are the lush green jungles of the world. They provide a home for more species of animals and plants than any other habitat on Earth.

Rain forests cover about 6 percent of the world's surface, but that figure is going down all the time. Every minute, about 2,000 rain forest trees are destroyed, which means hundreds of millions of trees are disappearing every year. In this book you can find out all about rain forests and what is being done to prevent their destruction.

What is a Rain Forest?
Rain forests are vast forests where it rains nearly every day and the temperature is always warm. This warmth and moisture make them ideal places for plants to grow.

From the sky, a rain forest looks like a huge green mass of broccoli tops, and all the trees look much the same. In fact, there are many hundreds of different kinds of trees growing side by side. Each large tree is home to many smaller plants that trail themselves over its branches.

Standing in a Rain Forest
If you visited a tropical rain forest you would find it a hot and steamy place. Your clothes would soon be damp, especially

From above, the rain forest looks like a mass of trees that are all the same, but there are many different kinds of trees in a tropical rain forest.

if you got caught in one of the daily showers of rain. The air would smell moldy because the ground is covered with rotting leaves. It would be quite dark and gloomy, too, since hardly any sunlight penetrates through the thick layers of foliage.

You would probably hear the screeches and calls of all kinds of wild animals above your head. More than half of all the known animal species in the world live in rain forests. Most of them live above ground, among the tree branches, where they can find food and shelter.

WHEN TREES DISAPPEAR

Rain forests are being destroyed by humans. People cut down the trees to sell the wood, to clear the land for farming, or to use it for mining, oil drilling, dams, or roads.

When the trees go, so do the homes of huge numbers of animals and plants. We could even be losing plants that might have provided us with powerful medicines against our worst

diseases *(see page 20)*. The destruction of the rain forest may also be contributing to world climate change, with serious results for everyone *(see page 8)*.

For these reasons, both scientists and politicians are making international efforts to stop the destruction. You can find out what you can do to help at the end of this book.

Workers use a bulldozer to clear this part of an Indonesian rain forest.

Where to Find Rain Forests

Most rain forests grow around the equator in an area that stretches around the middle of Earth. Here, day and night are of equal length and the Sun's heat is fierce all year long. The temperature is always hot, and rain falls regularly.

Jungles in this region are called tropical rain forests. A few rain forests grow farther away from the equator, in areas of Australasia and North America. These are called temperate rain forests. They have a great deal of rainfall but not year-round warmth.

South and Central America

The world's biggest tropical rain forest grows along the Amazon, one of the world's largest rivers. This forest stretches all the way across the middle of South America; a fifth of all the world's known plants and animals live there.

Central America was once completely covered in rain forest too, but more than half of it has been cleared over the years to make way for plantations and cattle pastures.

Asia

Asia's tropical rain forests stretch from India and Myanmar in the west to Malaysia in the east. They include the jungle-covered islands of Java and Borneo. In parts of southeast Asia, it is hot and humid all year round, but on mainland Asia there is a monsoon climate. This means that torrential rains fall at certain times of the year. This rainy season is followed by a drier season.

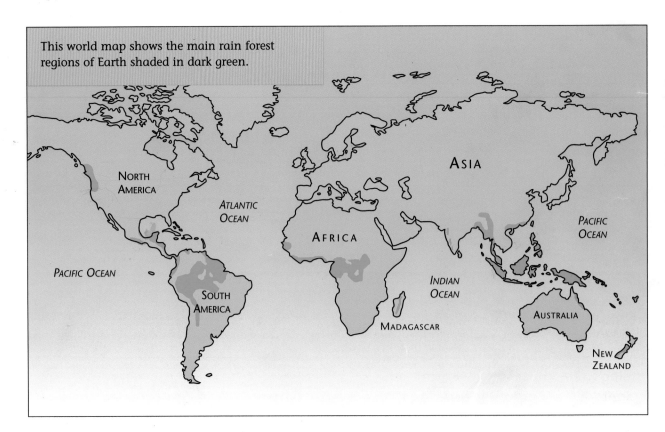

This world map shows the main rain forest regions of Earth shaded in dark green.

NORTH AMERICA

ATLANTIC OCEAN

PACIFIC OCEAN

SOUTH AMERICA

AFRICA

ASIA

PACIFIC OCEAN

INDIAN OCEAN

MADAGASCAR

AUSTRALIA

NEW ZEALAND

The world's second-largest rain forest region flourishes in Central Africa. Here, there are several different kinds of rain forest, including misty cloud forests and tangled mangrove swamps.

Mangrove swamps are a type of rain forest that grows in coastal areas, where the water is salty. The mangrove trees stand high on their roots, which act like stilts. The roots suck up the water but filter out the harmful salt.

Cloud forests grow in high places such as mountains. These forests are misty and the trees obtain most of the moisture they need from mist rather than from rain. Gorillas, the world's biggest apes, live in the African cloud forests of Uganda.

Off the southeast coast of Africa, the island of Madagascar is home to many unique rain forest plants and animals, including lemurs. Now, 90 percent of its forest is destroyed and the rest is in danger of disappearing in the next twenty years.

A mangrove swamp in West Africa. African rain forests are remote places that are difficult to visit and study.

Asia's rain forests are home to some of the world's most endangered mammals, such as the orangutan and the tiger. Fossil records show that these jungles have existed for up to 100 million years, but a third of them have disappeared since 1960. They are being rapidly cleared to create farmed plantations for crops such as oil palms.

Australasia

In parts of Australia, New Zealand, and Papua New Guinea, rain blows in from the Pacific Ocean. This helps create temperate rain forests that contain wildlife found nowhere else on the planet. Unusual creatures, such as the rain forest possum and the duck-billed platypus, thrive here.

Rain Forest Science

Important natural processes happen in the rain forest to keep the trees alive. Although these processes cannot be seen, they are vital. When they stop, there are serious consequences for the environment.

Water Recycling

Rain forest trees recycle rain. An amazing 13 to 20 feet (4 to 8 m) of rain falls on rain forests every year. Some falls on the trees' leaves; the roots soak up any that falls to the ground. The moisture travels up the tree trunks to the leaves; from there it is slowly released into the air by evaporation. Half of all the rain that falls on the Amazon rain forest returns to the sky this way. The water vapor gradually rises up into the air and forms rain clouds, which later drop their rain nearby. In the Amazon, it rains heavily three or four times a week, along with regular short thunderstorms.

Photosynthesis

The billions of leaves in the rain forest soak up sunlight like tiny solar panels. They also take in a gas called carbon dioxide, or CO_2, from the air. Leaves use CO_2 and light energy to make nutrients, which help the trees grow. At the same time, they also release the gas, oxygen, into the air. This whole process is called photosynthesis. So much oxygen is created by the rain forest that they have been called "the lungs of the world."

Cycling Nutrients

Trees need chemicals called nutrients to help them grow healthily. Rain forest soil is very low in nutrients because rain washed them away long ago. Trees, however, have their own way of creating a supply: When their leaves fall to the ground, they rot, putting nutrients back into the soil. The trees then absorb these nutrients through their roots.

CHANGING THE WEATHER?

Where areas of rain forest are cut down, water recycling stops. This shift may change the local climate: Water vapor is not released to form rain clouds, and instead of getting the regular rain they are used to, people living in nearby areas might find that there is not enough rain for them to grow their crops.

Burning rain forest wood could be affecting the climate of our entire world. When fuel such as wood is burned, carbon dioxide (CO_2) is released. Scientists have noticed that Earth's climate is warming up very quickly, a process they call global warming. Scientists believe that increasing CO_2 in the world's atmosphere helps cause global warming. We all need the protective blanket of gases — called the atmosphere — to create an environment where we can all thrive. Increased carbon dioxide in that blanket, however, prevents much more of the Sun's heat from escaping into space.

Eventually, as a result of global warming, the North and South Poles may melt and cause a rise in sea levels. To prevent this change from happening, people need to limit the amount of CO_2 they create. Cars, factories, and power plants produce a lot, but it is also estimated that at least one-fifth of the world's excess CO_2 is coming from people burning rain forest wood.

In the rain forest, rain usually falls in short and heavy bursts.

Rain Forest Layers

A rain forest tree is like a natural version of an apartment building: Different creatures and plants live on different levels. Trees rely on animals to spread pollen and seeds. Animals rely on the trees to provide food, such as juicy fruits and sugary nectar.

Overstory

The very top of the rain forest is called the overstory. Rain forest trees usually grow to around 164 feet (50 m) in height, but some trees stretch high above the others, up to 197 feet (60 m). These are called emergent trees.

Large birds, such as harpy eagles, sometimes use emergent trees as nesting sites and lookout positions. Emergent trees make a good place for birds of prey to spot their quarry in the branches below.

Canopy

Beneath the overstory, a dense layer of leaves and branches, called the canopy, spreads out. The canopy is the busiest section of the forest. Birds, small mammals, reptiles, frogs, and insects all live here, enjoying the canopy's rich store of fruit, flower nectar, and seeds. In a tropical rain forest, there are no actual seasons. Instead, each tree species flowers and fruits at its own particular time.

Understory

The understory is the area below the canopy, where the leaves and branches are not as dense, and much wildlife lives. In tropical rain forests, parrots fly around, and monkeys can sometimes be seen swinging from rope-like plants called lianas. Lianas look as if they are hanging down from above, but, in fact, they grow up from the ground.

An emergent tree is taller than the others in the forest. It makes a good perch for birds of prey.

Underneath rain forest trees lies a layer of plant material called leaf litter. In time, micro-organisms and fungi rot the leaf litter, and this process replenishes essential nutrients in the soil (*see page 8*). If you turned over some leaf litter, you might spot beetles, ants, or centipedes, because many insects live here. In contrast to these tiny creatures, some of the largest rain forest mammals also roam between the trees on the forest floor. In the Amazon, for example, large, pig-like creatures, called tapirs, snuffle around looking for food.

Many insects live in the rain forest. These leaf-cutter ants make their home in the damp layer of leaf litter on the rain forest floor.

Shrub Layer

At ground level in undisturbed areas, called primary forest, there is little sunlight, so the vegetation is usually quite sparse. Baby trees and bushes grow here.

Forest that has been thinned out by fire or by humans is called secondary forest. Here, more sunlight can penetrate to the shrub layer, and it tends to be more crowded, with different types of plants. It is harder to walk through the shrub layer in a secondary forest.

In the shrub layer, giant buttress roots splay out around trees to keep them standing up. These thick roots make a booming sound when they are kicked. In Amazonia, local people signal to each other by drumming on them.

Rain Forest Animals

Over 50 percent of the world's animal species live in the rain forest, and that is only counting the ones we know about. If you visited, you would hear animals screeching, calling, and trilling, especially at night, when many of the rain forest creatures are active.

Reptiles

The rain forest makes an ideal home for snakes and lizards because it is a warm climate with much food available. Tree snakes coil their way around the branches, looking for small creatures to eat. Lizards sit waiting to catch passing insects.

Some rain forest snakes are deadly poisonous to humans, or large enough to crush someone to death. For example, the world's heaviest snake, the anaconda, lives in the Amazon region. It can grow up to 30 feet (9 m).

Frogs

Much of the nighttime noise in a rain forest comes from tiny frogs calling to each other up in the forest canopy. They have sticky pads on their toes to help them climb. Many of them live in small pools of water that collect in bowl-shaped plants growing high in the trees.

Rain forest frogs are often brightly colored, which warns other animals that they are poisonous to eat. One of the strongest poisons produced by any animal comes from the tiny poison arrow frog, which is no bigger than a human thumbnail.

Mammals

Rain forest mammals range from tiny bats to big gorillas and tigers, and 90 percent of all the world's monkeys live in rain forests. There are many species of rodent, too, including the Amazonion capybara — the world's biggest rodent — which can grow to reach the size of an adult sheep.

A red-eyed tree frog in Panama, Central America, looks alert. Rain forest frogs are often brightly colored. They make lots of noise when they call to each other at night.

We may be losing fifty animal and plant species every day because of the destruction of the rain forests. This loss could cause serious problems in the future. Scientists believe it is very important that our planet has "biodiversity," which means it has as many different animal and plant species as possible to help keep all life healthy and thriving. Fewer species could mean that, over time, more diseases and harmful genetic defects could spread through the animal and plant kingdoms.

Birds

Roughly 30 percent of the world's birds live in rain forests. Vividly colored macaws and hornbills use their tough beaks to feed off a rich harvest of fruits and nuts in the trees. Tiny birds, including hummingbirds no bigger than bees, rely on flower nectar for nourishment.

Insects and Spiders

Many rain forest insects still remain to be discovered. Some scientists think that up to 90 percent of the world's insects may live in rain forest regions. Known rain forest insects range from giant beetles the size of a human hand and moths the size of dinner plates to tiny ants you need a magnifying glass to see properly. Scientists estimate that one rain forest tree provides a home for up to two hundred different insect types. The number of actual insects per tree probably runs into many hundreds of thousands.

Rain forest trees contain a wide range of spiders, too, ranging from aggressive hunting spiders to thousands of small spiders living together in colonies that hang in giant webs.

This brilliantly colored blue Morpho butterfly lives in a South American rain forest.

Rain Forest Plants

Rain forest plants vary in size from the world's biggest flowers to microscopic plants too small to see with the naked eye. They provide us with all kinds of food, flavorings, medicines, and other useful products, such as rubber.

Plants We Use

Bananas, peppers, okra, peanuts, and cashews are some of the familiar food plants that are grown in rain forest regions. Coffee and tea, oil palms, vanilla, sugar, and all kinds of spices are farmed there, too.

Tropical forest oils and gums are used in insecticides, rubber products, paint, varnish, cosmetics, and shampoos.

Most importantly, rain forest plant extracts are used in many modern medicines. For example, 2,000 tropical forest plants have been found to have some cancer-fighting

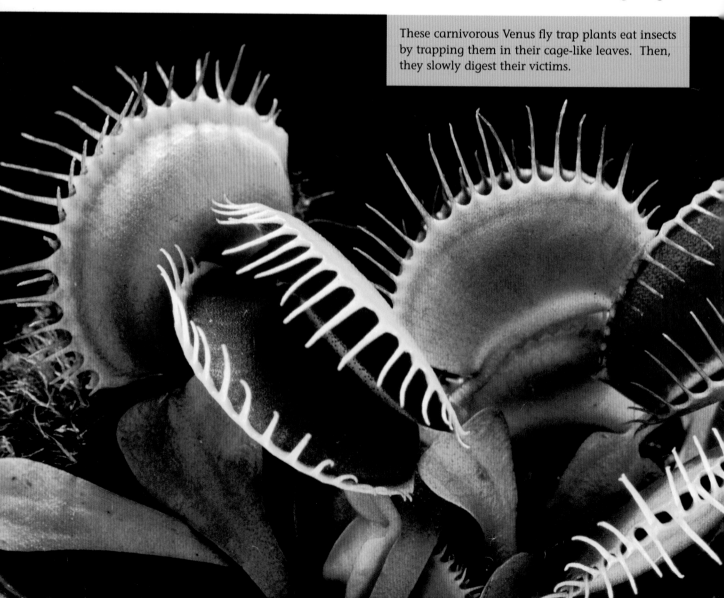

These carnivorous Venus fly trap plants eat insects by trapping them in their cage-like leaves. Then, they slowly digest their victims.

properties. So far, scientists have only tested one in ten of the rain forest plants they know about (*see page 21*). Many more beneficial plants could disappear before scientists ever get the chance to investigate their unique properties.

Killer Plants

Some rain forest plants are carnivorous, which means they eat meat. They trap small creatures and then digest them to

absorb nutrients. Some large carnivorous plants will even trap and eat small mammals and lizards. Another common rain forest plant is the strangler fig. It gradually grows up around a tree, suffocating it until it dies.

All about Epiphytes

Many rain forest plants are epiphytes, which means they dangle their roots in the air to get the water and nutrients they need. They grow on the branches and trunks of forest trees. Their seeds are dropped there by passing animals, or are blown there on the breeze.

Tropical orchids are epiphytes. There are thousands of different kinds, some so rare they are

worth a fortune to plant hunters. Bromeliads are rain forest epiphytes, too. They have thick, waxy leaves that form a bowl shape to collect rainwater for the plant to use. These little rainwater pools in turn provide a home for animals, such as frogs.

Useful Ropes

Lianas can grow to more than 3,000 feet (900 m) long. They hang between trees, helping to hold the trees up. Lianas begin life as seedlings on the forest floor and then attach themselves to small trees. As the tree grows, so does the liana. Animals such as monkeys use lianas to climb trees and travel around in the forest canopy. An Asian type of liana is called rattan. It is used to make baskets and furniture.

Fungi: Small but Vital

Some of the tiniest life forms in the rain forest are the most vital. Fungi and small plants send their roots into dead leaves and bark and help rot them down quickly, releasing nutrients into the rain forest soil.

How to Tap Rubber

Natural rubber is a useful rain forest plant product that can be collected without causing damage to the trees. To do this, a rubber collector carefully cuts into the bark of the rubber tree. Beads of creamy, white latex, the raw ingredient of rubber, seep out and dribble down into a bucket via a channel cut in the side of the tree. Collecting rubber this way is called "rubber tapping." Once heated in vats over fires, the sap becomes stretchy and is ready for sale to a rubber company.

Trees in Danger

A rain forest tree can take more than a hundred years to grow but only a few minutes to cut down. The large-scale cutting down of forests is called deforestation.

Logging

Much rain forest wood is called hardwood because it is tough and very hard-wearing. People pay a lot of money for it. Hardwood is used to make products such as furniture, flooring, ships, and strong packing cases. Unfortunately, the most valuable hardwood trees grow alongside many other species. When a logging company cuts down one profitable tree, it may destroy dozens of other healthy trees, leaving them to rot. To find enough useful trees, loggers may cut down many acres (hectares) of forest.

On a smaller scale, local people cut down trees to burn as fuel. Many people who live in rain forest regions are very poor and cannot afford to buy fuel. They can only get it by collecting it for free in the forest.

Farming

Most of the world's rain forests are in countries that have overcrowded cities and many poor people. To find free land to farm, people often follow the roads cut into the rain forests by loggers. Then they cut down the forests to grow food for themselves and their families. Rain forest soil is very thin, and, once the trees are gone, much of the soil is soon washed away by the rain. The ground quickly becomes useless for growing anything, so the settlers move on to cut down another area of forest.

Larger areas of deforestation are caused by commercial farming companies that clear land to make big plantations for profitable crops such as coffee, or to plant grass in order to graze cattle. The only way to keep the land fertile is for the farming companies to cover it regularly with lots of chemical fertilizers. Unfortunately, these fertilizers often wash into local streams and rivers, contaminating the water.

This factory in the Philippines produces elaborate carved furniture using wood from tropical forests.

PROFIT OR LOSS?

Mining, oil drilling, and damming are big business in rain forest regions. They also pose a big threat to rain forest environments. For example, when a dam blocks a river, it creates a giant reservoir of water behind it. The water is channeled through the dam to turn turbines that generate electricity. When the dam is built, the reservoir floods a large area of forest. To save time and money, the rain forest trees are sometimes left standing as a dam is built. Then the area is flooded, killing all the wildlife. "Scuba lumberjacks" then fell the trees underwater using diving equipment, so that the trees float to the surface to be taken away. If they are left in the reservoir, the trees gradually rot and turn the water into acid that pollutes the water.

Big rain forest projects such as mines, oil wells, and dams are very controversial. Organizations that try to protect the environment — and the rain forests themselves — point out that the profit these projects make does not take into account the cost of the damage they can do.

A section of Amazon rain forest that has been clear-cut for a dam project.

People in Danger

The rain forests of the world are home to "indigenous" peoples who have lived there for many centuries. As the forests are destroyed, their way of life is in grave danger.

Life in the Amazon Region

Amazonian Indians hunt for food in the forest and grow crops on agricultural plots. They clear a small area of forest to grow crops, which are carefully chosen and varied from year to year so as not to use up all the soil's nutrients. After a while, the Indians will move to another plot, leaving the forest to regrow, and causing the least possible impact on the natural life of the rain forest.

They also gather wild rain forest plants, which they use to make all kinds of useful things, such as food, medicine, dyes, soap, clothing fibers, and even insect repellent. There are thought to be several Amazon tribes living so deep in the forest they are not known to any outsiders.

Life in Africa

The Efe people make their home in the rain forest of Central Africa. They don't farm, but rely on the rain forest for their food. They hunt monkeys, birds, and rodents and collect food such as honey, nuts, and edible insects. When they hunt for honey, they use special whistles to make a noise to lure the bees away from their nests.

The tribe owns few possessions — just a few baskets, bows and arrows, and some simple homemade musical instruments. The African forests are being cleared, so the tribe's way of life is in great danger. In addition to this threat, the Efe people live in war zones: Many have been killed in the fighting.

Life in Other Rain Forests

The rain forest tribes of Papua New Guinea in Australasia and those of Borneo in Malaysia hunt and grow food, too. They were once fierce headhunters who shrank the heads of their enemies and displayed them in their villages as proof of their bravery. Now, facing the challenges of modern times, they battle against climate change, rain forest destruction, and water pollution caused by careless mining and oil production.

A TOUGH FIGHT

When rain forest tribes first met people from outside, catastrophe quickly followed. They had no natural immunity to the diseases carried by outsiders, and many thousands died from everyday European diseases, such as chicken pox and the common cold. Now there is a further threat to the existence of rain forest peoples. As loggers, miners, and settlers gradually move into rain forest regions, they often use violence to drive out the Indians. Rain forest tribes are not rich in material goods and have little political influence. They find it hard to resist the destruction of their societies and way of life.

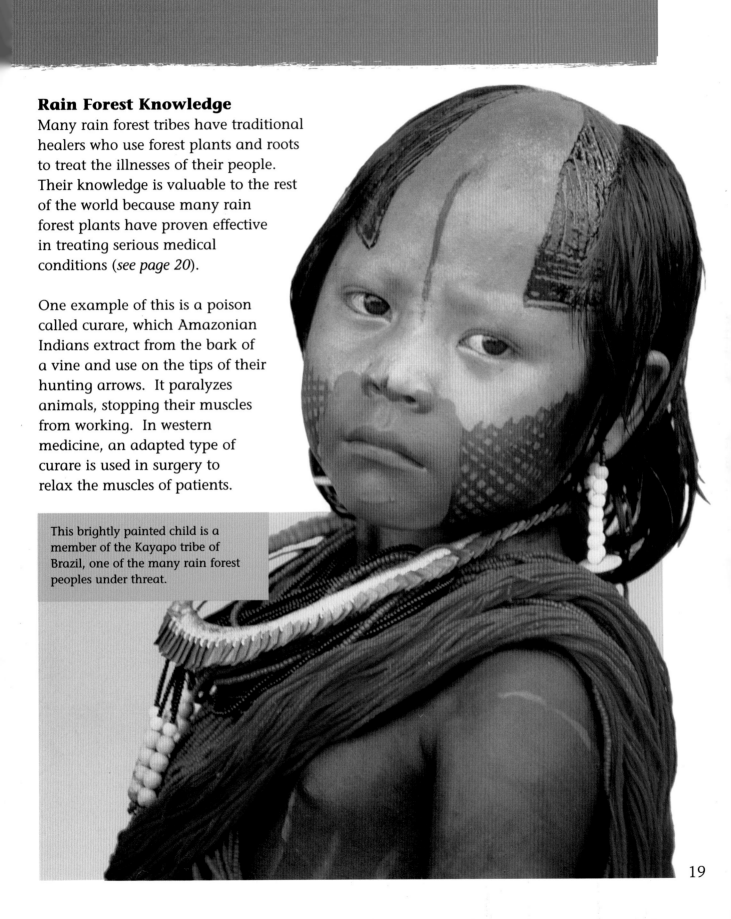

Rain Forest Knowledge

Many rain forest tribes have traditional healers who use forest plants and roots to treat the illnesses of their people. Their knowledge is valuable to the rest of the world because many rain forest plants have proven effective in treating serious medical conditions (*see page 20*).

One example of this is a poison called curare, which Amazonian Indians extract from the bark of a vine and use on the tips of their hunting arrows. It paralyzes animals, stopping their muscles from working. In western medicine, an adapted type of curare is used in surgery to relax the muscles of patients.

This brightly painted child is a member of the Kayapo tribe of Brazil, one of the many rain forest peoples under threat.

Saving Rain Forest Plants

In the long run, people may discover that the true wealth of rain forests will be found, not through selling its trees for timber or mining its ground, but through harvesting rain forest plants for medicine and food.

Good Rain Forest Business

Crops which are harvested but then re-grow easily are called sustainable. Sustainable rain forest crops include fruits, nuts, plant oils, and some species of trees. It has been calculated that an area of rain forest that is carefully looked after and harvested sustainably earns a lot more money over the long term than if it were simply cut down and sold as wood.

The World's Plant Store

Many of the foods we eat were originally discovered in rain forests. Mangoes, spices, bananas, coffee, chocolate, and vanilla are all familiar examples. Nowadays, these are mainly grown on big plantations, but the rain forests still house a store of different varieties that can be used to help keep plantation crops healthy. By crossing old plant varieties with newly discovered ones, farmers can produce new types of crop with built-in protection against diseases and weather damage.

Many foods are possibly yet to be discovered in the rain forest. For example, it is estimated there might be more than 3,000 different kinds of rain forest fruits; yet, so far, we only know about a few of them.

The Healing Forest

At the moment, about 25 percent of all western medicines contain substances that originated in the rain forest. So far, only about 1 percent of rain forest plants have been tested for medical use. Many cures for major illnesses still wait undiscovered in the rain forests. Many pharmaceutical

Rain forest trees and plants produce an astonishing variety of fruits and seeds.

SAVING THE SEEDS

The rain forests are like a giant library of plant species. Botanists are trying to catalogue this library and collect seed samples before this resource is destroyed. They go on field trips to the forest to collect seeds, which they take back to seed banks, which are run in the world's plant-studying centers. Here, the seeds are identified, cleaned, x-rayed to see inside them, and then dried and frozen.

They can be preserved this way for hundreds of years and will still grow again if planted. That means they could be re-introduced into the wild in the future.

To help identify the seeds, botanists bring home leaf samples, too. Kew Gardens, in London, has a seed bank with more than seven million pressed leaf samples stored with their seeds.

A scientist at a seed bank in Malaysia works on a conservation program for wild garlic.

companies are now sending botanists (people who study plants) to rain forest regions to discover unknown useful plants. They talk to local healers to find out what they use plants for. Then they collect samples and take them home for laboratory analysis and testing, to make certain that they are safe for human use. Rain forest plants are particularly rich in substances called alkaloids, which help protect them from diseases and insect attacks. Alkaloids make very effective human medicines, too.

Saving Rain Forest Animals

Many rain forest creatures are in danger of extinction, but the more we know about them, the more likely it is that we can find ways to save them. Here are some examples of how scientists are trying to help.

Last Chance for Orangutans

Orangutans are intelligent, gentle creatures, and the only apes that live in trees. Their natural home is on the Asian islands of Borneo and Sumatra, where the rain forest is fast disappearing and where the apes are illegally hunted. Now the orangutan species is dying out.

By observing wild orangutans and studying their habits, scientists can figure out how many there are left and how best to protect them. For example, they have discovered that orangutans can be moved to new areas of replanted forest, away from human settlements, if the right fruit trees are planted as food for them. The seeds of the orangutans' favorite fruits have been collected from their droppings and planted in these new areas to grow.

A big threat to orangutan populations is the illegal animal trade. Baby orangutans are in demand as pets, so conservationists visit street markets and animal dealers to rescue baby orangutans taken from the wild. The animals are often quite sick by this point, and they must be nursed back to health. They are taken to sanctuaries, where experts on orangutan behavior teach them the skills they need to survive in the wild — lessons their mothers would have taught them — such as building nests and finding food.

Gradually, the orangutans are encouraged to go out into the forest and, eventually, to live permanently back in the wild.

Some baby orangutans are taken from their mothers and sold as pets. The mothers are often killed.

Scientists fit a sedated tiger with a radio collar.

Big Cat Rescue

Big cats, especially tigers, are highly endangered rain forest animals. One way to check on them is for scientists to sedate them with tranquilizer darts and fit them with radio collars. The tigers can then be tracked to find out where they roam. By doing this, scientists have discovered that when forest is cut down, big cats are often left stranded in small remaining patches, unable to find mates or sufficient food. If this occurs, they tend to stray into human settlements, where they are seen as a danger and are shot.

One way scientists hope to save big cats is by establishing "green corridors," which are protected natural routes between different patches of rain forest. In Central America, biologists are hoping one day to create a "Panther Path" across countries to help save the jaguar. To plan for this, they are using radio collars to track jaguars and have set up cameras on likely jaguar paths to check to see if the cats use them.

Changing Minds

Many rain forest creatures are illegally kidnapped or hunted every year. Tigers are illegally killed so that parts of their bodies can be used in traditional Chinese medicine. Their bones, eyes, whiskers, and teeth are ground into pills and potions, which are thought to give people the animal's strength.

It is very hard to completely stamp out profitable criminal activity, but one way is to encourage local people to use their knowledge to save animals, not hunt them. Most wildlife rangers are good at explaining about their work to their own communities.

Saving Rain Forest Trees

How can we save the rain forest trees — or try to replace them if they are destroyed? Here are some methods that are being tried.

Replanting or Controlled Logging

Planting new trees does not recreate an old rain forest as it once was, but it does help stop the soil from being washed away. When botanists replant, they try to use tree species that have roots that will quickly spread out and help anchor the soil before it gets washed or blown away.

Another way to try to preserve the forest is to encourage new settlers to farm more like the native people, planting the right crops and moving their farm plots around so as not to exhaust the soil forever.

Sometimes, forests have controlled logging, which means that the loggers are allowed to cut small groups or strips of trees down instead of large areas. That way, a forest has more chance of long-term survival.

Rain Forest Tourism

Rain forest countries can make a good income by opening rain forest reserves to tourists. This is called *ecotourism*. Many people are willing to pay to visit such a beautiful plant- and animal-rich environment. National parks have been created by law in some rain forest areas. They are managed by governments to ensure that they are not destroyed.

Rain Forest Law

There are now international laws that outlaw the cutting down of endangered rain forest, the stealing of land from native people, and the poaching of rare animals. It is very hard to enforce these laws because rain forests are usually in isolated, difficult-to-guard areas. In addition, they are often in the world's poorest countries, places that badly need to earn the money they can get from selling their wood. These countries often have big international debts,

BRAZIL NUT SCIENCE

Brazil nuts are a very valuable crop. They earn over $40 million every year for South America. Brazil nut trees, however, cannot be grown in plantations. They will only grow and produce nuts in remote, undisturbed rain forest, surrounded by different tree species. The nuts are collected by local people, called *castanas,* who hunt for the best crops.

Biologists have been studying brazil nut trees in the Upper Amazon, to try to find out as much as they can about them. If they find ways to get a better harvest, they hope to persuade people

that there is more money to be made from collecting brazil nuts than from chopping forests down. Researchers studied 1,000 trees, counting every pod that fell. They opened lots of nuts, fitted a tiny magnetic strip inside each one, and closed them up again. Then they discovered that rodents called agoutis ate or buried the nuts around the forest, helping to spread the tree to new areas. The biologists used a magnetic detector to find the buried nuts and then recorded where new trees were likely to grow.

which is money they have borrowed from international banks and then must repay. Politicians, people in business, and environmentalists often argue over whether to cut rain forests for short-term profits or protect them, but there are some things that everyone can do to help to solve the threat to the rain forests (*see page 28*).

A worker collects Brazil nuts. The nuts are located inside the grapefruit-sized pods.

Collecting Knowledge

The more we know about the rain forests and what is happening to them, the more we can help save them. Here are some of the methods used to collect this vital information.

Satellite Images

We know that rain forests are disappearing because satellites are able to monitor them from space using instruments that gather information about Earth's surface. Satellites designed for this kind of work carry sensing equipment that can detect different types of radiation. Everything on the surface of Earth sends out or reflects some radiation, but different objects send out different amounts. Satellites measure

Satellite images help scientists to keep track of rain forest destruction and regeneration. In this picture, the light-colored areas are land that has been cleared.

the amount of radiation and transmit the data back to Earth, where computers process this information to make images that show features of the landscape in different colors.

Satellite images are detailed enough to show small-scale logging, farming, roads, and forest fires. Their sensitive measuring equipment can even be used to distinguish between different tree sizes and species.

Preventing Disturbance

Scientists who study the lives of tribal people are called anthropologists. Many work in rain forest areas, talking to local people and recording details of their lives.

Deep in the Amazon rain forest, there are thought to be about seventeen tribes who have not yet encountered outsiders. Many anthropologists believe it is better to leave them undisturbed because, once they meet outside people, they are likely to die quickly of diseases that are unknown to them, such as the common cold. Even so, these people are at great risk from illegal loggers and settlers arriving to take their land.

Researchers are trying to find traces of where these tribes live — while avoiding meeting them — in the hope that laws can be passed to protect their land and leave them undisturbed.

Preserving Plants and Animals

Scientists are also trying to save threatened rain forest animals and plants by collecting samples of each species and trying to keep the samples alive for the future. These sample collections are known as gene banks.

Some highly endangered rain forest animals now have such low populations that the only way to keep their species alive is to breed them in zoos. In the near future, the only tigers and orangutans left in the world may be the ones in zoos.

One day, it could be possible to use genetic science to produce more of these animals by cloning, but it is not yet certain whether that will be realistic — at the moment, the science of cloning is in its infancy. Sadly, it is too late for many rain forest species that have already disappeared from our world.

RAIN FOREST CRIME BUSTING

Smuggling rare animals from the rain forest makes big money. It is estimated that up to twelve million Brazilian wild animals may be bought and sold illegally every year. Out of every ten animals captured, only one is thought to survive to reach its destination, usually as an exotic pet. The rarest creatures make the most money. A blue macaw parrot might sell for $25,000 and an endangered tamarin monkey for $20,000.

Customs police try to investigate and arrest the criminal gangs who capture and then sell the protected animals of the rain forests. They also try to find out who buys the animals from the gangs. The police may talk to contacts and hunt around local markets in rain forest areas, or run investigations on pet shops and Web sites. When possible, they try to rescue and return the animals to the wild.

What Can You Do?

Here are some suggestions for ways that you can find out more about the rain forests of the world and help to stop their destruction:

Watch What You Buy

Try to avoid buying things made of tropical hardwoods. That way you will be helping to reduce the number of trees cut down. The main types of wood to avoid are mahogany, teak, and rosewood.

It is hard to find out exactly where products come from and how they have been produced, but look carefully for any information on the packaging. Watch for the words "sustainable source," which means the harvesting of the crops is being properly managed to try to preserve the environment.

Cattle farming in rain forest areas has led to deforestation because the land is cleared for grazing. It is estimated that for each hamburger produced from cattle grazed on cleared land, over 55 sq feet (5 sq m) of forest has been destroyed. Try to find out where the meat you eat comes from by asking in restaurants or writing to your food companies.

When your family goes shopping, suggest that everyone should make an effort to buy goods produced by companies that are committed to saving endangered environments. Look out for fair trade products, too. When you buy these items, a fair amount of money goes back to the farmers who originally grew the crop. You can buy fair trade coffee, chocolate, and bananas from rain forest regions.

Recycle Your Stuff

Try to use recycled paper when you can, and make sure you recycle the paper that you no longer need. In the long run, this can help reduce the number of trees being cut down.

Recycling uses less industrial energy than making a new product and helps to cut down global warming. Find out how you can recycle your tin cans, bottles, and cardboard, as well as paper.

You could make some posters encouraging your family and your classmates to recycle things.

Don't Buy Exotic Animals

Do not buy rain forest animals as pets. You will only be encouraging criminals to catch more of them for profit. The animals are better off in the wild.

Get Involved

There are many programs run by recognized conservation charities that involve children and school classes in conservation projects. For example, you might want to help save an orangutan or a tiger. Ask your teacher if your class could become involved with a conservation charity. Here are some useful Web site addresses to help you start:

rainforest-alliance.org/index.cfm
Discover how to choose products that will help sustain the rain forests, discover more about this alliance's many projects, look at their nature photos, and more.

www.bagheera.com/inthewild/van_anim_gorilla.htm
Learn about gorillas and what is being done to protect them.

www.kidsplanet.org
Learn about the Endangered Species Act and the endangered animals under its protection.

www.nationalgeographic.com
Use the search words *rain forests* to discover all sorts of rain forest information, and take a virtual tour of a rain forest at night.

www.panda.org
Find out more about this organization's international work and environmental success stories on this Web site of the World Wildlife Fund. Use the search words *rain forests* to find articles about their ongoing work

www.papaink.org/gallery/home/artist/display/57.html
Gain consumer information and learn more about peaceful consumer actions that have helped save the rain forests.

www.tropical-forests.com/
Find maps, facts, and projects for you to try; book purchases through this site provide a donation to a charity of the International Children's Rainforest Network.

Glossary

alkaloid
a natural substance that protects plants from disease and insect attack

anthropologist
someone who studies the lifestyles and customs of people

biodiversity
the wide variety of living things on the Earth, providing a rich gene pool

botanist
someone who studies plants

bromeliad
a rain forest plant with thick, waxy leaves that grow in a bowl-like shape

buttress root
a tree root that grows above the ground and helps the tree stand firm

canopy
a thick layer of leaves and branches high up in the rain forest trees

carbon dioxide (CO_2)
a gas that is released when fuel, such as wood or coal, burns. It is also breathed out by animals in respiration and absorbed by plants in the process of photosynthesis.

climate
the weather and temperature usually found in an area

cloud forest
a tropical mountain forest that gets most of its moisture from mist rather than rain

deforestation
the destruction of trees over large areas

ecosystem
a natural system, also called a web of life, that includes all the living things in a particular area

ecotourism
tourism aimed at benefiting local environments, not damaging them

emergent tree
very tall rain forest tree that towers above the others around it

environment
the world around us

epiphyte
a plant that dangles its roots in the air to get the moisture it needs

fungi
tiny plants that do not photosynthesize, but instead get the food they need from dead leaves and rotting bark

gene bank
a collection of endangered plants and animals kept in storage or captivity in hopes of preserving their species

global warming
the warming of the world's climate, possibly caused by too much CO_2 in the atmosphere

hardwood
the tough, hard-wearing timber from rain forest trees, such as mahogany, rosewood, and teak

humidity
warm, damp air

indigenous
a living thing that belongs naturally to an area

leaf litter
a layer of rotting leaves on the floor of a forest

liana
rope-like plants that grow up trees

mangrove
a kind of rain forest tree that stands high on stilt-like roots and can live in saltwater swamps

nutrients
minerals that plants take from the soil to help them grow; substances which provide nutrition for living things

overstory
the very top layer of the rain forest

photosynthesis
the process by which green plants take in sunlight, CO_2, and water to make oxygen and food

plantation
a large farmed area of one crop, such as coffee or sugar

primary forest
forest that has never been cut down

recycling
turning waste into something that is reusable, rather than adding it to a landfill

secondary forest
forest which grows back after primary forest has been cut down

seed bank
a store of seeds kept in frozen conditions to preserve the seeds for study and future use

sustainable crop
a crop that can regrow quickly enough to allow it to be harvested on a regular basis

temperate rain forest
a rain forest that grows in a part of the world where there are cool and warm seasons

tropical rain forest
a rain forest that grows near the equator, the area that stretches around the middle of Earth. Here the climate is always warm.

understory
the area between the ground and the thickest layer of leaves (the canopy) of a rain forest

Index